Horsham Township Library
435 Babylon Road
Horsham, PA 19044-1224
215-443-2609
www.HorshamLibrary.org

EDGE BOOKS

TRUE TALES OF SURVIVAL PRESENTS:

LOST AT SEA!

TAMI OLDHAM ASHCRAFT'S STORY OF SURVIVAL

by Matt Doeden

Consultant:
Al Siebert, PhD
Author of *The Survivor Personality*

Capstone
press®
Mankato, Minnesota

Edge Books are published by Capstone Press,
151 Good Counsel Drive, P.O. Box 669, Mankato, Minnesota 56002.
www.capstonepress.com

Library of Congress Cataloging-in-Publication Data
Doeden, Matt.
    Lost at sea!: Tami Oldham Ashcraft's story of survival/by Matt Doeden.
    p. cm.—(Edge books. True tales of survival)
    Includes bibliographical references and index.
    ISBN-13: 978-0-7368-6780-1 (hardcover)
    ISBN-10: 0-7368-6780-5 (hardcover)
    ISBN-13: 978-0-7368-7878-8 (softcover pbk.)
    ISBN-10: 0-7368-7870-X (softcover pbk.)
    1. Ashcraft, Tami Oldham, 1960– —Juvenile literature. 2. Shipwrecks—Pacific
Ocean. 3. Survival after airplane accidents, shipwrecks, etc.—Juvenile literature. I.
Title. II. Series.
G530.A757D64 2007
910.9164'9—dc22
2006030653

Summary: Describes how Tami Oldham survived at sea and eventually reached
    the Hawaiian Islands after her boat was destroyed by Hurricane Raymond and
    her fiancé was tossed overboard and lost at sea.

Editorial Credits
Mandy Robbins, editor; Jason Knudson, designer; Wanda Winch, photo
    researcher/photo editor

Photo Credits
Bruce Coleman Inc./Norman Owen Tomalin, 19
Corbis/Neil Rabinowitz, 10–11; Morton Beebe, 24–25
Getty Images Inc./Aurora/Michael Eudenbach, 14–15; Stone/John Lund, cover
Photo courtesy of Tami Oldham-Ashcraft, 4, 6, 8, 12, 13, 17, 20–21, 22–23, 26–27, 28
Shutterstock/Dan Collier, 1; Denver Steiner, 8–9 (background); dubassy,
    4–5 (background); Kezzu, 18–19 (background); Mark Bond, 28–29 (background),
    32 (background); Merrill Dyck, 6–7 (background); NSilcock, 16–17 (background),
    30–31 (background); Popovici Ioan, 2–3 (background); Riddle Photography,
    back cover; Robert Kyllo, 18

1 2 3 4 5 6 12 11 10 09 08 07

TABLE OF CONTENTS

CHAPTER 1

ADRIFT AND ALONE

LEARN ABOUT:

- A RUDE AWAKENING
- LOST LOVE
- INNER STRENGTH

Tami and Richard shared a passion for sailing. They lived on Richard's boat, *Mayaluga*.

They had been hit by a terrible hurricane.

On October 13, 1983, Tami Oldham woke up alone and confused on a battered yacht. The ship's cabin was a mess. As the 23-year-old stood, salt water came up to her knees. She was dizzy and had a bloody cut on her forehead.

Slowly, Tami's memory returned to her. She was in the middle of the Pacific Ocean. Tami and her fiancé Richard had taken a job delivering the yacht *Hazana* to San Diego, California. But during their trip, they had been hit by a terrible hurricane.

Tami awoke to complete chaos and destruction on *Hazana*.

Tami hurried to the ship's deck to search for Richard. During the storm, Richard was attached to *Hazana* by a safety harness. But now the harness clip was broken. That clip was all that could have stopped Richard from falling into the raging sea. Tami screamed his name, scanning the water around her. She threw flotation devices overboard, hoping Richard would find them.

Outside, the water was calm, but the damage to the ship was severe. Supplies were scattered everywhere. The mast poles that once held the sails were destroyed. The ship's main sails were also ruined. The radio antenna had washed away, and the engines were dead. *Hazana* was adrift, and there was nobody to help. Worst of all, Richard was gone.

A part of Tami was ready to give up. She thought about rolling off the edge of the ship to join her beloved Richard. But another part of her wanted to live. Tami Oldham began making plans.

CHAPTER 2

SETTING SAIL

LEARN ABOUT:
- A LIFE AT SEA
- AN INCREDIBLE OFFER
- SAILING INTO A STORM

Richard built his yacht, *Mayaluga*, himself.

Tami and Richard decided to sail around the world together.

Growing up in San Diego, California, Tami had always loved the sea. After high school, she moved to Mexico to live a carefree life on the beach. Later, Tami took a job on a yacht. She quickly grew to love the life of a sailor. She also discovered her talent for refinishing the outer surface of yachts.

While working as a yacht refinisher, Tami met Richard Sharp. The couple fell in love and got engaged. Richard owned a small ship named *Mayaluga*. Tami and Richard decided to sail around the world together.

9

Before they began their journey, their friends Peter and Christine Crompton made them an offer they couldn't refuse. For $10,000, Tami and Richard would deliver the Crompton's yacht, *Hazana*, from the South Pacific island of Tahiti to San Diego. The large amount of money was only part of the attraction. Tami and Richard would also have a chance to spend time on a bigger, fancier ship than *Mayaluga*.

A RISKY DECISION

Richard and Tami were eager to begin their journey. They left Tahiti on September 22, 1983, a few weeks before hurricane season ended. The weather forecasts looked good. The couple felt confident that they could steer around any storms that developed. Richard and Tami planned to be in San Diego in about a month.

11

HURRICANE RAYMOND

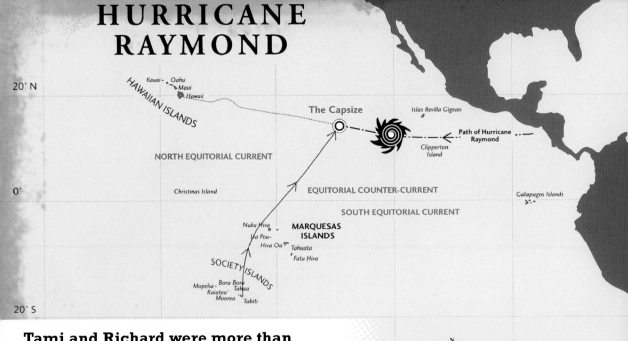

20° N

Kauai • Oahu
HAWAIIAN ISLANDS • Maui
• Hawaii

The Capsize

Islas Revilla Gigeao

Path of Hurricane Raymond

Clipperton Island

NORTH EQUITORIAL CURRENT

0°

Christmas Island

EQUITORIAL COUNTER-CURRENT

Galapagos Islands

SOUTH EQUITORIAL CURRENT

Nuku Hiva
Ua Pou • **MARQUESAS ISLANDS**
Hiva Oa • Tahuata
• Fatu Hiva

SOCIETY ISLANDS

Mopelia • Bora Bora
Raiatea • Tahaa
Moorea • Tahiti

20° S

Tami and Richard were more than halfway to San Diego when they crossed paths with Hurricane Raymond.

Early on, the sailing was going slow. The winds weren't blowing as Tami and Richard had hoped. One of their radios short-circuited. Then the ship's wind speed indicator stopped working. It was a bad start, but worse was coming.

12

On October 9, Tami and Richard learned of a tropical storm developing over Central America. Tropical Storm Raymond grew into a hurricane, and it was headed *Hazana's* way. Richard changed their course to miss the storm. But Raymond's path changed. Again, it was headed right at them. And this time, there was no time to get out of the way.

13

Richard's last entry in *Hazana's* log book read, "All we can do is pray."

AN ANGRY SEA

On October 12, Hurricane Raymond hit *Hazana*. The storm's powerful winds blew up waves as high as a four-story building. The yacht was built to stand up to rough weather, but Raymond was just too much. As Richard fought to keep the ship afloat, he sent Tami below deck to keep an eye on the weather instruments.

Once below, Tami secured her safety harness. The violent crash of waves made moving around almost impossible. But Tami soon felt a moment of stillness that told her *Hazana* had fallen into a deep trough. Tami knew a huge wave was about to hit.

From above, Richard shouted, "Oh my god!"

The wave smashed into the yacht, violently throwing the ship to one side. Supplies flew about the cabin. Something hit Tami in the head, and everything went black.

If Tami had stayed on deck during the hurricane, she probably would have died.

CHAPTER 3

LIMPING TOWARD LAND

LEARN ABOUT:
- **WAKING UP TO A NIGHTMARE**
- **MAKING A SAIL**
- **LONG LONELY JOURNEY**

Tami awoke to discover that the ship was in ruins and Richard was gone. Fearing that *Hazana* would sink, she loaded supplies into the life raft. But a gust of wind blew a whole bag of supplies overboard. It was almost too much for Tami to take. She dropped into the life raft, still on the ship's deck, and slept.

16

When Tami awoke, Richard was nowhere to be found.

Canned sardines were one of the foods Tami ate on her long journey.

ON THE MOVE

The next day, Tami realized that *Hazana* wasn't going to sink. Richard may be dead, but she was alive. Tami started making plans to survive. Fresh drinking water was her first concern. Luckily, Tami discovered that one of the ship's tanks was half full of fresh water. She also had some canned food.

Using the ship's medical kit, Tami cleaned and bandaged the gash on her forehead. She then looked at *Hazana's* charts to figure out where she was. She guessed that she was about 1,500 miles southeast of Hawaii. The winds and ocean currents would make those islands her best destination.

19

Tami directed *Hazana* to Hawaii using a traditional sailing tool called a sextant.

Tami knew where she wanted to go. But with the main sails torn, she had no control of the ship. The ship's masts had been snapped, and the engines didn't work either. Tami found a spinnaker pole, which is used to secure a large sail. She set up the pole to work as a mast and attached her last remaining sail to it. The sail was small, but it was enough to catch some wind. *Hazana* was moving again.

A LONG VOYAGE

The days and weeks that followed felt long and lonely. Tami spent her time steering the ship and thinking about Richard. Her days became routine. She ate, drank, and steered the yacht.

The highlights of her days were taking measurements of the sun using a tool called a sextant. Sailors mark the exact time the sun is at its highest point and when it hits the horizon. They use the times to figure out a ship's position. These calculations kept Tami on course for Hawaii and told her how fast she was moving.

On good days, Tami sailed up to 60 miles (100 kilometers). Other days, she barely moved at all. With her little makeshift sail, it was slow going. All the while, Tami fought against loneliness and depression.

Once during her voyage, Tami fastened ropes around herself and dove under *Hazana* to check the ship's rudder. She rewarded herself by eating a can of fruit.

Without Tami's knowledge of sailing, she would have drifted in the ocean until someone found her.

EDGE FACT

Tami thought she had been knocked out for three hours during the hurricane. But when she reached Hawaii, she realized that she was off by a day. She'd actually been unconscious for 27 hours.

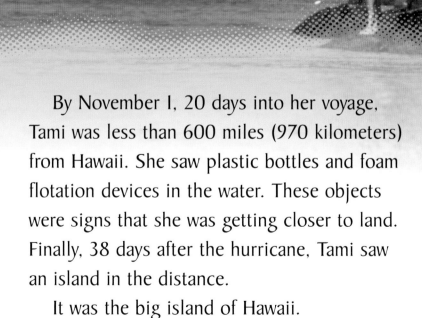

When Tami saw the island of Hawaii, she knew her navigation skills had saved her life.

By November 1, 20 days into her voyage, Tami was less than 600 miles (970 kilometers) from Hawaii. She saw plastic bottles and foam flotation devices in the water. These objects were signs that she was getting closer to land. Finally, 38 days after the hurricane, Tami saw an island in the distance.

It was the big island of Hawaii.

CHAPTER 4

SAFE HARBOR

LEARN ABOUT:
- **SOLID GROUND**
- **BITTERSWEET REUNION**
- **LIFE GOES ON**

26

The ship that towed Tami was a Japanese research vessel called *Hokusei Maru*.

Early in the morning of her 42nd day alone, Tami was just outside Hilo Harbor. She spotted a ship's lights in the distance, grabbed her flare gun, and shot a flare. She watched the ship change its course to meet her. Tami knew that she was going to be rescued.

SOLID GROUND

The crew members of the ship wanted to help Tami in every way possible. After calling the Coast Guard, they threw her a line so that they could tow her toward the harbor. They also tossed her a thermos of hot coffee and an apple.

Tami's mother flew from San Diego to Hawaii the day after Tami was towed into Hilo Harbor.

The Coast Guard brought Tami into the harbor. She spent the night at the home of one of the Coast Guard officials. There, she made tearful phone calls to her grandparents, mother, and father.

MOVING ON

Tami's story of survival became global news. After she returned to San Diego, Tami did a TV interview for *CBS News*. She stayed a while in San Diego and then went to England, where Richard was from. There, she met with the Cromptons and Richard's family to tell them about his heroic death.

After losing Richard, it took Tami a long time to move on with her life. Nine years after the shipwreck, in 1992, Tami married Ed Ashcraft. The couple lives on San Juan Island in Washington with their two children. Tami often speaks at yacht clubs, and she and her family continue to sail. Despite her frightening experience, Tami Oldham Ashcraft still loves the sea.

GLOSSARY

flare (FLAIR)—a burst of light shot from a gun to announce one's presence or position

harbor (HAR-bur)—a place where ships load and unload passengers and cargo

hurricane (HUR-uh-kane)—a strong tropical storm that includes heavy rains and very strong winds

mast (MAST)—a tall pole on a ship's deck that holds its sails

sextant (SEKS-tahnt)—an instrument that uses the distance between the horizon and the moon, sun, or stars to determine a ship's location at sea

spinnaker pole (SPIN-uh-kuhr POHL)—a long, light pole that secures a sail called a spinnaker

trough (TRAWF)—the low point between two waves

yacht (YOT)—a large boat or small ship used for sailing or racing

READ MORE

Ashcraft, Tami Oldham. *Red Sky in Mourning: A True Story of Love, Loss, and Survival at Sea.* New York: Hyperion, 2002.

Riley, Peter D. *Survivor's Science in the Ocean.* Survivor's Science. Chicago: Raintree, 2005.

Todd, Anne M. *Sailing Adventures.* Dangerous Adventures. Mankato, Minn.: Capstone Press, 2002.

INTERNET SITES

FactHound offers a safe, fun way to find Internet sites related to this book. All of the sites on FactHound have been researched by our staff.

Here's how:

1. Visit *www.facthound.com*

2. Choose your grade level.

3. Type in this book ID **0736867805** for age-appropriate sites. You may also browse subjects by clicking on letters, or by clicking on pictures and words.

4. Click on the **Fetch It** button.

FactHound will fetch the best sites for you!

INDEX

32